Stay Home,
Stay Safe

At first, Kevin was happy when it was announced that schools were closing due to the pandemic. Covid-19 was a serious matter; taking many lives and everyone needed to take safety precautions to slow down the virus. Everything was shutting down, including schools. Kevin loved waking up and logging on to his computer in his pajamas. His parents were working from home, so they all sat down to eat breakfast each morning. After breakfast either parent found time to go over Kevin's schoolwork with him.

Everyone thought the new changes were temporary and soon all would be back to normal. After a month of homeschooling, Kevin was ready to get back into the classroom to see his friends and teacher.

Another month passed by and Kevin was growing tired of staying at home. The first few months after it was announced that the country had to stay home and if they went outside of their homes, they had to wear a mask, Kevin only left the house a few times to join his parents whenever they went to the grocery store. And on those few times, he waited in the car. Soon his parents could see that he was struggling with staying home, so they thought of some creative things he could do, and also things that they could do as a family.

Kevin's father approached him with some ideas that could make learning from home fun. "Kevin, each morning before you log onto the computer for class, you should video chat with some classmates. It's a great way for you to catch up with them and see how they are dealing with being at home during this pandemic," his father suggested.
"That's a good idea Dad," Kevin let him know.

Kevin chatted with friends every morning and they were all excited to see one another on video. He saw that some of his friends got new animals to play with while they were stuck in the house. One girl got a parrot who loved to interrupt their conversations. It was funny for Kevin to hear a parrot saying full sentences. Another friend got a gerbil who seemed to love joining in on the video chats.

With Kevin being the only child, it could get lonely, so he thought about asking for a dog. He brought the idea up to his parents, but they did not think he was responsible enough yet to care for a dog. They got him a fish tank and filled it with all kinds of fish. They had him write an essay on the names of each fish and what parts of the world they were mostly found in. The fish tank was filled with guppies, swordtails, flower horns, angelfish, and goldfish. The fish were beautiful and Kevin loved doing the research on them. He was responsible for feeding them and keeping the tank clean.

Kevin's mother gave him another suggestion to stay in touch with classmates. "Kevin, one day a week we can have one of your friends over for an hour. But the both of you have to keep a mask on the entire time."
"That sounds great Mom," Kevin told her.
Kevin let his classmates know what his mother suggested. A few of his friend's parents were still concerned about the virus, so they declined. But there were a few whose parents agreed and brought their kids by to play with Kevin. They

only had an hour to visit, so they usually played a video game.

Kevin's mother came up with another idea. She knew there were kids whose parents could not afford to buy masks, so she bought a sewing machine so that Kevin could help her make some colorful designed face masks. Kevin was excited to come up with designs for some of the masks. He came up with so many great ideas that his mother let him take control over designing all of the masks. He used different Disney characters and superheroes. His classmates loved them and wore them during on-line classes just to show them off. The teacher thought it was a great idea and told other teachers, so Kevin was asked to make masks for their students, as well.

The teachers put together a fund for the materials to make the masks so that Kevin's parents did not have to absorb all of the cost. Kevin found himself busy designing and making hundreds of masks.

The media heard about it and wanted to do an interview with Kevin and his parents. After they did the interview, calls poured in for him to make masks for other neighborhoods and schools. This led to his parents to start a small business making masks for sell. They showed Kevin how to open a bank account and keep inventory of how many masks he made and how many sold.

Kevin was busy! His business was so profitable that his parents put most of the proceeds into a college fund for him and with a portion of the money left, Kevin donated to a local animal shelter.

Kevin's teacher missed her students and did weekly visits at each of their homes for any assistance they needed. He was always excited whenever she visited. She knew some of her student's struggled learning through the on-line classes, so she wanted to make sure none of them were falling behind in their work.

No one expected that schools would shut down for the remainder of the school year. Once the numbers were rising in Covid-19 cases, his parents thought it was best that no one came to the house, so he was really missing his friends. It looked as though it was going to take some more time before things went back to normal. They knew Kevin was bored. He was doing well feeding the fish and keeping the tank clean. He also fulfilled all of his orders for the masks and saved a lot of the money. They were proud of him, so they planned a surprise for him.

The morning Kevin's parents were going to surprise him, he was not feeling well. His mother took his temperature and he had a fever. She panicked and called his doctor. She was afraid that Kevin may have Covid-19 and the doctor asked her was he having any other symptoms. He was not, so the doctor told her not to worry too much and to give him some cold medicine to see if his fever goes down. The medicine worked.

Once Kevin fully recovered from being sick, he better understood why his parents were being cautious about allowing his friends to come to the house. They were grateful it was not serious, and planned to continue wearing a mask and washing their hands often, and whenever out of the home to stay at least six feet away from people.

It was time for Kevin's surprise. His parents took him to the same animal shelter where Kevin had made a generous donation. Kevin was so surprised when his parents told him to pick a puppy. There were so many to choose from that he was having a hard time deciding.

His parents saw that he was confused on which puppy to choose, so they pulled him outside.

"Kevin, I know it's hard deciding on which dog you want because they all are so adorable. But see which one you think will be the easiest to train by asking him or her to sit or lay down," his mother suggested.

They went back in the pet store and the first three dogs that Kevin asked to sit, all sat. Then he asked them to lay down and one out of the three laid down. That was the puppy he took home.

Kevin soon learned that taking care of a puppy was a lot of work. The hardest part was training his new puppy, Max to go to the bathroom outside. Max was confused. He seemed to always play outside and go to the bathroom inside. His parents saw him struggling and suggested that he not allow Max to play so much whenever he took him outside, and to put him in his cage each time he wet the floor. Hopefully, Max will quickly learn that he cannot go to the bathroom inside the house. His parents hoped Max would be fully trained soon because they grew tired of helping Kevin clean up after him.

Once Max understood where to go to the bathroom, he was a joy to have in the home. Kevin was happy that he got to be home with Max during the pandemic. It made it easier to get Max on a schedule to eat, play and take walks outside.

It was almost a year into the pandemic and schools were still closed, hospitals were full to capacity, restaurants closed, people were still working from home, and masks were required everywhere you went. It was a scary time and Kevin worried about the possibility of him and his family getting sick. Although they were following all of the safety precautions, the reports still showed high numbers of people infected with the virus. He knew making the masks helped contributed to people being safe, but he just wanted to do more.

After hearing about so many people losing their jobs, Kevin talked to his mother about doing a food drive.

"Kevin, we know you want to help, but I don't think it's a good idea to do a food drive right now due to the rise in Covid-19 cases," his mother warned him.

"I'll wear my mask the entire time and I'll ask everyone who comes to wear their mask," he promised her.

"Let me talk it over with your father and see what he thinks. I know there are probably many people who need a helping hand during these times and any help will be greatly appreciated," his mother replied.

Kevin's parents agreed that as a family, they would do a food drive in their neighborhood, so they made flyers to pass out.

On the day of the food drive, they set up two tables to collect the food. They were surprised at how many people in their community and beyond showed up with boxes and bags filled with food. There was so much that Kevin's father had to rent a truck to hold most of it. "Kevin, this was a great idea," his father told him.

"Yes, it was," his mother agreed, "the local food bank will appreciate this help."

"Why did they bring pet food?" Kevin curiously asked.

"Because those people who lost their jobs most likely have a pet, and pets have to eat too," his mother explained.

"I didn't think about that," Kevin said.

"I am so proud of you, my son. We knew you were bored and missed your friends, but not once did you complain. We all hope things go back to normal, but until then, we have to make the best of a bad situation," his father proudly stated.

"Thanks Dad," Kevin replied.

"And to add to what your father said, I am proud of you, as well. You not only helped people, but you learned how to run a small business and how to save money. This pandemic has been an awful experience. I'm glad that we stuck together and did not let it stop us from helping others and staying strong as a family unit," his mother added.

"Thanks Mom. I couldn't have done it all without the both of you. I do miss my friends and family.

I especially miss going to see Grandma on the weekends," Kevin said.

"She's been missing you and needs someone to help set her up on the computer so that she can video chat with you," his mother said.

"I'll call and see if her neighbor can set her up on the computer," his father said.

The next morning Kevin got a surprised call from his grandmother. She learned how to set up a facetime call. They both were teary-eyed as they got through their first conversation since the pandemic seeing one another.

Kevin and his grandmother stayed on the phone for over an hour. When they hung up, Kevin's parents could see that he really missed her.

"Kevin, there's a vaccine out that has been promising in getting rid of the virus, so soon everyone will get this vaccine and things can finally go back to normal. The good thing is they will give it to the elderly first, so once your grandmother gets it, we'll pay her a visit," his mother told him.

"That will be great. I know she's lonely since grandpa passed and I worry about her," Kevin tearfully responded.

His mother hugged him.

"We worry too. We'll take a drive very soon to see her. Her neighbor checks on her daily," his father assured him.

A month later Kevin got to see his grandmother. She got vaccinated and could not wait to see her family. The family also had a Covid-19 test done and they tested negative. Kevin went to the market and bought fruits, sweets, and toiletries for his grandmother. He was so proud that he had the money to do these things for her.

His grandmother cooked dinner. After dinner, Kevin knew that his grandmother had a special dessert for him. She always baked him some sort of cake. This time she made a strawberry short cake.

"Kevin, I want to thank you for the thoughtful items you brought me. And I want to say how proud I am of you. Your parents told me that you started a small business making masks and how you donated your money and time to helping those less fortunate during these dangerous times. You are a wonderful grandson," she told him.

"Thank you Grandma. I really missed you and I am so glad I finally got to see you. I was worried about you," Kevin admitted.

"I understand your concern since your grandpa is no longer here, but my neighbors check on me often. I love my house; it holds a lot of memories. Yes, it gets lonely sometimes living here alone, but I wouldn't want to be any place else," his grandmother confessed.

She got up to grab an old photo album. The first picture she showed him was a picture of her holding him as a baby.

"This is one of the memories I cherish. We had the extra bedroom turned into a nursery when you were born. Then we added the playground in the backyard so you had a place of your own to play. Then added the tree house so you had a place to get away. We had your first birthday right in that backyard. This house means everything to me. So, don't you worry about me being here alone. I sit in every room and remember all the great times had in this house," she said, and smiled.

Kevin continued to facetime with classmates and his grandmother. Even though he wanted to go outside and play, or go over friend's houses, he was no longer sad about staying home because he knew the severity of the crisis our nation was in. His parents continued playing board games with him, they took walks together along with Max, and they ate dinner together every evening. Overall, some good things came out of the pandemic for their family.

Kevin was getting used to wearing a mask and was actually enjoying it because he was wearing a variety of them. He made one to match all of his outfits and did the same for his parents. He even made some for his grandmother and her neighbors. And because his parents felt he was taking all of the necessary safety precautions to stay safe, they trusted him to go outside and play while wearing his mask. He rode his bike around the neighborhood and took the dog on longer walks.

Spring was approaching and Kevin's mother asked him to help her plant a garden of flowers. He agreed and she let him pick the flowers. They planted orchards, tulips, daisies, and lilacs. Kevin could not believe little seeds could grow into beautiful flowers. It did not take long before each plant started sprouting.

Kevin's mother saw that he was excited to see how seeds grew into flowers, so she had him help her plant herbs. They planted sage, oregano, dill, parsley, thyme, basil, mint, and rosemary.

"Wow, these are a lot of herbs!" he said with excitement.

"I use all of these herbs whenever I cook. Most are used in just making my famous spaghetti sauce," his mother said.

"This one has a funny name. How do you pronounce it?" Kevin asked while holding up the packet of seeds for Thyme.

"It's pronounced time, but they spell if different," his mother answered.

"What do you use it for?" Kevin curiously asked.

"Sometimes I use it whenever I bake chicken," his mother answered.

Kevin held up the pack of mint to his nose and sniffed it.

"I love the smell of this one," he said.

"That's mint, and I use it to make tea," his mother said.

"This one sounds like a woman's name, Rosemary," Kevin chuckled.

"It sure does," his mother agreed and smiled.

After they planted the herbs, Kevin was treated to a big bowl of chocolate ice cream for helping his mother. As he enjoyed his ice cream, he thought about all of the fun had while staying home, and all the things he learned. He got to see his parents more and spend a lot of fun time with them. He learned how to make masks and run a small business. And with the business, he learned how to save money. He learned to help those who were suffering during the pandemic by giving back and having a food drive. The fun things he did was planting flowers and herbs, spending one day a week playing video games with classmates, and learning how to sew. The best gifts were the fish tank and his puppy, Max. But one gift topped them all... the time he spent with his grandmother. It was priceless.

To see more books, go to:
www.lisajoybooks.bigcartel.com

Send a message to the author about the book!
lisajoybooks@gmail.com

Made in the USA
Columbia, SC
01 December 2022

72464945R00015